THIS BOOK BELONGS TO

_____

Dedication

This book is dedicated to anyone who

is in need of a solution to a problem.

The answer may just be in you.

KIP

THE 'COPTER
AND THE
RUSHING RIVER RESCUE!

WRITTEN BY
SARAH JIBRIN

ILLUSTRATED BY
ALJON & NOVA INERTIA

Kip the 'Copter loves to explore.
He spends each day flying over Telotown
and learning all he can.
Although Kip the 'Copter is new in town,
everyone has come to know him as he flies overhead.

A favorite part of Kip's day is watching friends
and families spend their day outdoors.
What a great day for a picnic and playing in the park!

On sunny days, Kip joins Bo, the ferryboat,
while he awaits the arrival of the blue whales.

Oh, look, here are some now!
Kip and his friends on the boat are excited
to see the mother and baby whales.

On this particular day, something in the distance catches
Kip's eye as he flies high over the mountains.
He focuses and realizes it's Mr. McKay waving at him

"Hello, Mr. McKay!" Kip shouts, "is everything okay?"

"Please help me, Kip," Mr. McKay hollers back,
"My canoe is damaged and I'm stranded!"

"I will certainly help, Sir. Just wait right there,
I'll be back!!" says Kip.

As Kip flies back to the city, he wonders who he might ask to help rescue Mr. McKay.

Just then, he sees Bo-the ferryboat in the distance. "Of course," Kip realizes, "Bo can help!"

"Hurry, hurry, Bo! Mr. McKay needs your help.
He's stranded in the mountains by the Rushing River.
You are a boat, you can help him, right?"

Concerned for Mr. McKay, Bo thinks about how
he can possibly help him in the mountains.
However, he realizes, maybe he
isn't the vehicle for the job.

"I'm sorry Kip, I would love to help Mr. McKay,
but I'm a deep-sea only boat. If I go,
I'll get stuck in the shallow river, I'm just too big.
You'll have to find someone else to
help Mr. McKay," explains Bo.

This makes Kip feel sad, but he understands Bo's challenge.
He doesn't let that stop him though,
Kip thanks Bo, then hurries off to search for another way.

"Ah! Ha! Since a deep-sea boat won't work,
because the water is too shallow and rocky,
I'll see if a construction machine can do the trick!
Those folks can drive over any ground!"

With much anticipation,
Kip makes his way to the construction site.

As Kip arrives at the construction site,
he turns on his loudspeaker so the noisy machines
can hear him while he asks,
"Can any of you construction vehicles help Mr. McKay?
He is stranded in the mountains by the Rushing River,
and I know you guys can help him!"

Concerned for Mr. McKay, the machines discuss how they can help, but soon realize they are not a practical solution.

"We would love to help, Kip, but we're all too big to get through the forest on the way to the Rushing River," Christy Crane explains. "If we tried, we would knock down all the trees along the way."

This makes Kip feel discouraged, but he understands the construction vehicles challenge. Still hopeful, Kip continues his search for the perfect vehicle for the job.

"I got it! Since a deep-sea boat won't work, because the water is too shallow and rocky, and the construction vehicles can't do it because they'll knock down the trees, I'll ask Jenica, my friend the passenger jet! She won't have to fuss with the water or land at all! She is strong, fast, and can fly to Mr. McKay to help him!"

AIRPORT

Kip flutters to the airport and thankfully,
he finds Jenica at her gate.

"Jenica, I'm so glad you're here! Mr. McKay
is stranded in the mountains by the Rushing River.
You are strong, fast, and can carry people.
Would you be able to rescue him?"

Jenica takes a moment to consider how she can help. She then explains, "I'd love to help Kip, but I can only fly very fast in one direction and I'd need a runway, which won't be available on the mountains. I'm just not built for that sort of thing - there is no way I could do it."

Again, Kip receives sad news. "It seems like no one can help Mr. McKay," he says to himself.

Just as he was about to continue his search, Jenica shouts, "Hey Kip, come back! There is a way to do it!"

"Oh, did you think of a way you can help Jenica? That would be great!" Kip says with hope restored.

"I can't, Kip – but you can! Think about it!

As a Helicopter, you can hover and fly in any direction

up,

down,

side-to-side

forward

backward.

You can fly over the water, pass over the trees,
and you won't even need a place to land. You are the solution
to help Mr. McKay. You are the one who can rescue him!"

Kip thinks about it for a moment,
"Wow, I can do it, can't I?"
Kip says with wonder.

Eager to get to Mr. McKay,
Kip flies through the mountains
to the Rushing River as fast as he can.

"Mr. McKay! Put the safety harness on,
grab the ladder and help yourself in,"
Kip shouts as he arrives.

Mr. McKay does as Kip instructs and climbs up the ladder
with all his strength.

Kip lifts him up carefully and cranks up the ladder.
Mr. McKay hops safely inside the helicopter,
and they head home.

Once they land, Mr. McKay shows Kip much gratitude.
"Thank you for rescuing me, Kip!
How can I ever thank you enough?"

"No need, Mr. McKay. I am glad I was able to help!" said Kip.

That night, as Kip thinks about his day,
he is filled with happiness,
knowing that Mr. McKay is safe.

It had never occurred to him that he could rescue someone.
It's nice to know he's just as helpful and valuable to the
town as Bo, the construction vehicles, and Jenica.
As he looks at his new home, Kip smiles, thinking of all
the ways he'll be able to help his wonderful new friends
in Telotown, because, after all, sometimes the solution
to a problem lies within you.

Paperback ISBN: 978-1-955668-13-2

Ebook ISBN: 978-1-955668-14-9

Library of Congress Control Number: 202192184

BOOK ENDEAVORS

About the Author

Photo Credit: Simcommedia

Sarah Jibrin is excited to share with you her first children's book, which was birthed while inventing a bedtime story for her children.

It is important to Sarah that we take advantage of the opportunities we have with children to empower them to see their value and live with integrity. She hopes to contribute to your child's growth through this story and others to come.

Sarah lives in New England with her husband and children with whom she loves to spend time. She believes that it's never too late to be like Kip and discover the unique qualities that enable us to strengthen those around us while using our talents.

To keep up with Sarah, please visit: www.telotownadventures.com

About the Illustrators

"Team Inertia" is Aljon and Nova, a young couple inspired to create illustrations for children's storybooks. Aljon specializes in creating beautiful, one-of-a-kind illustrations.

His goal and purpose in life are to bring his passion for art to children's stories that speak to good morals and values while providing lessons for today's youth. His colorful illustrations bring engagement to the author's content, so the story comes alive on the pages.

Aljon's extraordinary work is featured in children's books worldwide.

Nova teamed up with Aljon to do freelance projects. She began with basic coloring, then fell in love with the creative process. At 25, with a new career as an artist, Nova didn't realize that her art skills were way beyond what she had ever imagined. She's found her purpose in the art industry.

Acknowledgments

My children who inspired this book – you have so much joy
and eagerness to know more.
You light up every room you enter and fill it with life.
Never stop asking questions; never stop expecting anything less than excellence.
I want to keep showing you all I know, give you everything I possibly can,
and walk with you on your journey, right by your side.

My husband, Michael – you help me let go, jump in with both feet,
and not be afraid. I fight you every time, but you continue to
patiently and steadily keep the message plain and simple, "do it."
Thank you for taking the fear out of me.

My book team, Teresa and Aljon – I loved working with you both on this project.
I greatly appreciated your enthusiasm for my story and the pleasant
side conversations we shared along this journey.
I hope to work with you both again.

My brother, Tim – your creative input means a lot to me.
I see you as having the ultimate creative gift to outshine us all on anything you touch.
Thank you for your support and for taking the time to help me refine this story.
Your input gives me a boost that this thing may actually be all right!

Kip and Friends Word Search

```
M V V G W S F P Z A Z T Z P J T T W V U J U A Z
E J X Q W H J H P X W A C A N K T E L O T O W N
Q Y R N B F T O U N I O D S R W R F I U Y P G O
L A G Q S K W W D J O B P S P T M A D Q F U W M
J T Z D K Y S I W X Z Y C E K Z K J M J N A S H
H D Q O N O D Z I W P R R N C R F Y D Y L K N B
P Z R R O L O K B T V R W G Q S J U I L S K I B
M N H E Z E R R L G U E V E W P N E A W N V A X
C E W H L G P P O Z U F Y R P X O B N N V H T E
H H U Q H A T N W T Q O V J V L O R G I G Q N R
X E R C W G Y D I L A B T E U A U K O U C K U E
D H S I S G L V N J S V L T T L U D S G T A O V
U E Z V S E Z P A U B H A W D Y H E D X T S M I
C L K U Q T R L Q Q L A H C O I D W U E Y G H R
V P I Z T N Y S C I S A P V X I U O J F H P E G
C A M Q P W Y C L Z L G B U R E I X H R T W L N
W Q T K G U G N R E N P Q B W X E K I I F J I I
Z R J N P R N V Y A Z E P O M H K I N E C N C H
X E W F G M N O G Z N U X Q G R I L D N N H O S
X I Z K O K U H B O E H V S F M S D D D L P U
H G U I A C P U U F Z S M V I U W C A S E V T R
G F Y P A Q T V I J Y Q G M B B Z I K N F M E Q
A I Q N J F P D T D U M P T R U C K O A F M R E
C O N S T R U C T I O N M A C H I N E S Y K E L
```

All Aboat Whale You Can
Bo Ferryboat
Christy Crane
Construction Machines
DT Dump Truck
Eddie Excavator

Friends
Helicopter
Help
Hero
Jenica
Kip

Mountains
Mr. McKay
Passenger Jet
Rescue
Rushing River
Telotown

Words can be forward, backward, diagonal, up and down

Need some help? Go to TelotownAdventures.com for the answer key

Made in the USA
Middletown, DE
22 December 2021

55997349R00020